For Henry and Theodore
—C.W.

For Robin, whose laughter still resonates
in our ears and whose bright light shines
on in our hearts
—W.H.

Text copyright © 2019 by Caroline Wright

Jacket art and interior illustrations copyright © 2019 by Willow Heath

All rights reserved. Published in the United States by Rodale Kids,

an imprint of Random House Children's Books, a division of Penguin Random House LLC, New York.

Rodale Kids and colophon are registered trademarks of Penguin Random House LLC.

Visit us on the Web! rhcbooks.com

Educators and librarians, for a variety of teaching tools, visit us at RHTeachersLibrarians.com

Library of Congress Cataloging-in-Publication Data is available upon request.

ISBN 978-1-9848-5014-0 (trade) — ISBN 978-1-9848-5015-7 (lib. bdg.) —
ISBN 978-1-9848-5016-4 (ebook)

MANUFACTURED IN CHINA

10 9 8 7 6 5 4 3 2 1   First Edition

LASTING LOVE

Caroline Wright

illustrated by
Willow Heath

RODALE
KiDS

Something very beautiful
and strange happened
when Mama was told
she was sick.

She came home from the hospital
with a magical creature.

The creature is strong,
like the strongest part of her.
The part that loves me so much.

The creature helps her be Mama every day,
no matter how bad her body feels.

We are cozy together.

We are inspired together.

Together, we find beauty everywhere.

Our creature rests and grows stronger,
even as Mama slips away.

After Mama is gone,
I have never felt more alone.

And then our creature finds me again.
As it turns out, he never left.

He became part of our family.

The creature is always by my side now.

He never tries to cheer me up.
He just keeps me company.

He still holds that strongest part of Mama
and helps me find her every day.

With him, I am never lost.

Together, we still find beauty.
Together, we find Mama everywhere.

Author's Note

Even though I was told I had a year to live after my cancer diagnosis, I didn't feel like I was dying. It was too surreal. Despite my strength and profound hope for survival, I thought of all the lessons I wanted to teach my children— everything from wearing their seat belts to always being kind to each other. The message in this book, however, is the one essential truth that really matters, a truth that provides comfort to any of us facing an uncertain future: a parent's love is forever. This belief transcends time and mortality. In this light, I knew we would all be okay, no matter what came along.

I wrote this book for my boys, and I am endlessly grateful to be here to read it to them.

—Caroline Wright